About the Author

Born in Sydney, Australia, Brady was trained as a graphic artist working on *The Sydney Morning Herald* then for a smaller publishing company, *Modern Magazines*. He formed his own art company, Bazza Art, designing publications including *Movie Magazine* for The Greater Union Organization, the largest distributor of films in Australia. He also self-published a magazine titled *Reelin' and 'Rockin*. Dealing with '50s and '60s rock'n'roll movies, it became "the Bible" for journalists researching the subject. Brady was also lead guitarist and vocalist with his group "The Ramrods" - the '60s band managed by ex-prime minister, Paul Keating.

The Galactic Adventures of Stella Starlust: Defender of Truth, Justice and the Milky Way

Brady Styles

The Galactic Adventures of Stella Starlust: Defender of Truth, Justice and the Milky Way

Olympia Publishers
London

www.olympiapublishers.com
OLYMPIA PAPERBACK EDITION

Copyright © Brady Styles 2023

The right of Brady Styles to be identified as author of
this work has been asserted in accordance with sections 77 and 78 of
the Copyright, Designs and Patents Act 1988.

All Rights Reserved

No reproduction, copy or transmission of this publication
may be made without written permission.
No paragraph of this publication may be reproduced,
copied or transmitted save with the written permission of the publisher,
or in accordance with the provisions
of the Copyright Act 1956 (as amended).

Any person who commits any unauthorized act in relation to
this publication may be liable to criminal
prosecution and civil claims for damage.

A CIP catalogue record for this title is
available from the British Library.

ISBN: 978-1-80439-019-1

This is a work of fiction.
Names, characters, places and incidents originate from the writer's
imagination. Any resemblance to actual persons, living or dead, is
purely coincidental.

First Published in 2023

Olympia Publishers
Tallis House
2 Tallis Street
London
EC4Y 0AB

Printed in Great Britain

Dedication

I dedicate this book to my wife, Patti. Robert and Johnny are still right.

Episode 1

**MOONLIGHT
BECOMES YOU**
- It goes with your fangs

or

On the night vein to Jugular Bite

Chapter 1

'The difference between ordinary and extraordinary is that little extra.'
— Jimmy Johnson.

A warm, gentle breeze caressed her silky, blonde hair as the beautiful young woman walked slowly along the beach. It was the time of day she liked Waikiki best, the hour just preceding dinner and the quick tropical darkness. The shadows cast by the tall coconut palms lengthened and deepened. The light of the falling sun flamed on Diamond Head, tinting with gold the rolling waves sweeping in from the coral reef.

Just tall enough to be majestic, with a figure whose curves set men's pulses hammering, Stella Starlust moved with feline grace; her penetrating blue eyes shone with that intangible something that lends allure to some fortunate women. The corners of her mouth curved into a smile as she kicked playfully at the lapping water with her bare feet. For the first time, for as long as she could remember, she felt at peace with the world.

Then, suddenly, her tranquility was shattered. From somewhere in the distance she heard her name being called. It was a strange voice; it became louder. She stopped walking, straining to hear the words. A cold hand touched her shoulder. The words were now pounding her eardrums.

"Wake up, Starlust. In case you did not remember, today is your birthday. As is customary on such an occasion, I would like to wish you, Happy Birthday."

Stella was jerked from the depths of a sound sleep with an abruptness that left her breathless. Propped upon one elbow, she forced her eyes to focus. "Thank you, Randy." The words came out as a gravelly whisper. She cleared her throat and managed a sitting position. "How long have I been asleep?"

"Exactly twelve hours, seventeen minutes and twenty-three seconds. I have prepared a glass of champagne for you to celebrate this… special time."

"That's extremely thoughtful of you."

"I am programmed to be extremely thoughtful, Starlust, along with numerous other human qualities, as you are fully aware."

Accepting the glass of bubbly, Stella cocked her head to one side. She spoke calmly but there was a subtle gleam of annoyance in her eyes.

"I've lost count of how many times I've asked you to stop calling me 'Starlust.' You know I prefer 'Stella.'"

"I do comprehend. However, the name 'Starlust' has an odd pleasurable effect on my circuits." Randy turned away, hesitated a few moments then added, "despite the fact this is your birthday, I would appreciate you covering, what is referred to as your 'Birthday Suit.' Your nakedness appears to be the direct cause of my central electrodes overheating."

Stella shook her head and smiled. "Randy, there are times when I wonder where the dividing line begins and ends between your robot and human characteristics." She slipped into a filmy, blue kimono, took another sip of champagne then joined her companion on the control deck of her spaceship, the Euphoria.

"I perceived that you were dreaming just before I woke you," Randy said.

For a moment Stella's eyes glazed as she recalled segments of her dream. "Yes," she replied wistfully, "I was dreaming of... my home... back on Earth." She closed her eyes, opened them then sighed. Gulping the last of the wine, Stella moved to the view scope and gazed out at the sweeping blackness of infinity – so impressive, so mysterious.

"This is not a question a woman would normally ask," Stella said without looking at Randy, "but, do you know what age this day has, unceremoniously, dragged me into?" She held out her empty glass. "Before you answer, would you be so kind as to pour me another and, on second thought, lie a little about my age."

"I anticipated your request." Randy handed her another glass. "But you know I am incapable of falsifying the truth. Due to this fact, and in answer to your question, based on Earth's time constituents, today you have entered your thirty second year. To verify this, simply subtract thirty-two years from this day's date, which is the second of August 2214, and you have the year of your birth – 2182 AD. During that year, Earth went through –"

"Yes, yes, I know all that!" Stella snapped.

After a moment of silence, Randy said, "I sense traces of displeasure in your voice, Starlust. It was not my intention to upset you."

Stella smiled. "You didn't upset me, Randy. It's just that... this is the second birthday I've had aboard the

Euphoria and, at times, I yearn for the simple pleasures that are a part of being… home. To see the carpet of the waters, apple-green by day, crimson and gold at sunset; to marvel at the brief tropic dusk as it dims the bright colors of Waikiki with the island lights trembling along the shore; to feel the trade winds playing with your hair as they blow across the Islands out of the cool northeast." She turned back to the view scope. Her eyes were misty. She stared at the black void fretted with hordes of stars above, below, in every direction, and felt, as she had many times before, the crushing magnitude of the universe.

Above the constant hum of the spaceship's mechanism, Stella heard Randy say, "I understand." It was enough to ease her tension. Moving away from the view scope, she raised her glass. "Spoken like a true friend, Randy. Here's to you." She watched the bubbles dancing in the yellowish fluid. "And… Happy Birthday to me." She took a sip then a smile flitted across her lips.

Agent Stella Starlust, accompanied by Randy, the latest product in state-of-the-art robotics technology, spent the past seventeen months aboard her beloved spaceship, the Euphoria. Through years of intense training, under the guidance of Earth's best masters of mind and body discipline, Stella's mental and physical capabilities have been enhanced to an almost super-human level. Due to her extraordinary aptitudes, she was chosen by the United Space Commission for a two-year assignment as an interplanetary troubleshooter.

Her immediate superior was Commander Cranston Lamont. Although constantly exasperated by Stella's rebellious attitude and her insistence on wearing provocative outfits, Lamont had the greatest respect for her abilities – and a deep affection for her. However, this radiant beauty, despite her astonishing expertise, was only human – strong yet vulnerable, exceedingly intelligent yet capable of making mistakes. And, although generally proficient at controlling her emotions, there were times when her heart got in the way of her mind.

But, right at this moment, Stella's mind was focused on a more important situation. She had just received a distress call from Carpathe, a small planet on the outer edge of the galaxy.

"We're back on duty, Randy." Her eyes sparkled with excitement. She threw off her kimono and headed to where she kept her small collection of 'working attire.' "I suppose I'd better get dressed."

Randy gave a low, metallic sigh. "I would appreciate it, Starlust."

Chapter 2

The deep throb of the Euphoria's powerful engines gradually faded into silence as the ship came to rest in an open field. Stella told Randy to stay aboard until she needed him. Following directions contained in the communication, from a Dr. Hal Vensing, Stella easily found her way to their meeting place, a small inn, The Frog and Toad, on a dimly-lit, cobblestone street.

Heavy black, slow-drifting clouds threw the whole scene into an eerie diorama of light and shade as they sailed across a bright full moon. This tiny village of Paprika burgh, one of only a few on the planet, reeked of gloom. As usual, the clammy sky was like an oppressive shroud wrapped around the tops of the tall surrounding mountains. But tonight, in particular, the loneliness of evil hung thick in the air.

Dr. Hal Vensing was a tall, slender man, finely-featured, and with a friendly manner. His hair and carefully trimmed moustache were deep black. As his sharp eyes, wrinkled at the corners, watched Stella walking toward him, he felt a mixture of admiration and anxiety. He forced lightness as he spoke.

"Thank you for responding so quickly, Agent Starlust," he said.

Stella nodded. "There was urgency in your message. What seems to be the problem?"

"Let's go inside." Vensing swung the pub door open.

"We can talk safely in there."

As they entered, a sudden hush fell over the few customers of the quaint establishment.

"They don't seem to take too kindly to strangers," Stella commented softly.

"I think it's probably your outfit that's left them speechless," Vensing replied.

"What's wrong with it?"

"It's just that there's not much of it," Vensing said then smiled. "Not that I'm complaining. I like it. Or, rather, what's in it."

They headed to a table far enough removed from the others with the hope of achieving a degree of privacy.

"May I get you a drink, Agent Starlust?" Vensing asked.

"I like the way you do business," she said with an impish grin. "Yes, thank you, I'll have champagne, if that's possible in this joint. And, please, call me, Stella."

Vensing smiled. "Call me, Hal. Make yourself comfortable. I'll get our drinks."

The moment Stella sat down the low drone of conversation again filled the premises. It wasn't until they'd almost finished their second glasses of wine that Vensing finally gained the courage to answer Stella's initial question.

"During the past month, two teenage girls have been murdered and six others have been reported missing."

"What is the local police force doing about it?"

"Nothing," Vensing said. "They left town, too afraid to stay."

"Why?"

A frown wrinkled Vensing's pleasant features. "You'll

probably find this difficult to accept," his words were almost a whisper, "but I believe, as do the rest of the village folk, the one responsible for the murders and, possibly, the missing girls, is... a vampire named, Count Dal V. Lucard."

Exercising self-control, Stella sat calmly watching the few bubbles in what remained of her champagne. She swirled the liquid a couple of times then finished it in one swallow. Placing the glass gently on the table, she then stared directly into Vensing's eyes. He held her gaze. Stella possessed the instinctive ability to know when any one was lying. She was convinced Vensing was telling the truth. Or, at least, believed in what he felt was the truth.

Stella ran the tip of her tongue slowly around her full lips as she continued to look deep into the doctor's clear brown eyes. The movement with her tongue was an unconscious idiosyncrasy that sent a shiver of excitement racing up and down Vensing's spine.

Finally, Stella said, "what proof do you have that this Count Lucard is... a vampire, and is also responsible for the killings and abductions?"

Vensing shook his head and looked away. "I have no proof, only a gut feeling. It's just that these horrific occurrences only began after the Count moved into that abandoned, godforsaken castle up there in the mountains. He claims the castle belongs to him. He can have it – no-one else will go near it. Folks around here are convinced that it's haunted." He looked up, saw Stella's searching look and quickly added, "not that I normally believe in ghosts and demons but... there's something about the Count that is... evil. Will you please help me prove that I'm right?"

Stella studied Vensing for a while. She liked him. She

believed him. He was as scared of the Count as every other person here seemed to be. But he was brave enough to stay and try to eradicate this problem. She made a decision, one she hoped she wouldn't regret.

"Unfortunately, Hal, as you said, you have no proof. In spite of this, and don't ask me why, I *will* stay and do whatever I can to assist your cause. However, if Count Lucard turns out to be nothing more than an innocent, reclusive nobleman, then I cannot be responsible for any legal problems that may arise. If we charge in, vilifying and accusing, and we're wrong, I'll be suspended – indefinitely."

On an impulse, Vensing leaned across the table and kissed Stella gently on the lips. He pulled away, slightly embarrassed. "I'm sorry."

"Don't be, I liked it. Is there more where that came from?"

He leaned over again and kissed her with such passion she had to force herself not to reach down and take hold of that particular swollen part of his anatomy that had attracted her adoration from the moment they'd met.

She reluctantly released his lips. A seductive smile curled the corners of her mouth. "When the time is right," she said, lustfully eyeing off the bulge in his pants, "we may, hopefully, pursue the pleasures of the flesh. In the meantime, there is much work to be done."

Chapter 3

On the outskirts of the village, a vehicle pulled up outside the local graveyard. The young male driver switched off the ignition and turned to his attractive female passenger. "How is this, Honey," he said, licking his lips, "secluded enough for what you have in mind?"

The girl's eyes were wide. "I don't like it here, Larry." Her voice was trembling. "Let's go somewhere else."

The boy laughed. "Don't worry, Carla, the dead can't hurt you."

"But... "

"No buts!" His words had an edge of impatience. "Let's get down to you and me stuff."

"Well, all right." She reluctantly undid her top, revealing her small, soft breasts, their nipples beckoning. The boy began to feverishly lick, suck and smother them with kisses. She moaned softly as he slid his hand under her tight dress, eagerly edging up her thighs until his fingers found the moist, parted lips of her love passage. She reached over, undid his pants and released his already fully-erect tool of coition. Another soft moan escaped her lips. Leaning down, she licked the tip of his swollen member and was about to close her mouth around it when she thought she heard something scratching outside the driver's door. She stopped, looked out into the darkness but could see nothing.

"Did you hear that?" she whispered.

"Hear what?" Frustration was now in his voice. "I didn't hear a thing. Now, get down there and do what I love you to do."

Deciding she must have been imagining the noise, Carla shrugged it off. Taking hold of Larry's firm shaft, she wrapped her lips around it and began to work her charm on him. She could feel he was fast approaching the brink of an orgasmic rush when, from outside her door, she heard the scratching sound again. She suddenly stopped. Larry swore. But, this time, he had also heard the scratching. A cold shiver ran up his spine. He felt the hairs on his arms and the back of his neck stand on end. Unfortunately, his sexual urge was doing quite the opposite.

Deflated, and just a little scared, he somehow managed a brave front. "You stay here, I'll check outside. It's probably a branch. The wind could be causing it to brush against the door."

But there *was* no wind. Carla knew it and Larry knew it. Stepping slowly out of the vehicle, he looked around but could see nothing. The air was still – unnaturally still. The boy was breathing heavily, his heart pounding. He held his breath, hoping it would help him hear something, anything. There wasn't a sound. He was about to check outside Carla's door when, out of the corner of his eye, he thought he saw a movement. Before he realized what had happened, a large, black-clad figure sprang upon him. Larry felt steel-like claws ripping at his throat. He was powerless against the strength of the massive creature. It kept tearing at his neck, ripping off chunks of flesh. His clothes were drenched with his own blood. He tried to cry out but couldn't – there was nothing left of his throat. From inside the vehicle, he heard Carla screaming. It was the last sound he would ever hear.

Walking alongside Vensing, listening to him talk about the pros and cons of living on this strange little world, Stella was feeling an increasing attraction toward him. She was also aware that she couldn't allow herself to become too romantically attached – her assignment didn't permit it. Still, an amorous dalliance here and there couldn't do any harm, could it? She smiled when she imagined what the answer would be if she asked Randy: "If that is what you so desire then, please, do not tell me about it. Think of my electrodes."

"Something I've noticed, Hal," Stella remarked, slipping her arm through his, "Paprika burgh's wonderful old-world charm bears a remarkable resemblance to many 19th century Transylvanian villages back on Earth."

"It is interesting you mention Transylvania," Vensing said. "I have been doing a great deal of research recently on Earth folklore relating to vampires – in particular, the legend of Dracula."

"But Dracula was nothing more than a fictional character, the central figure of a tale written way back in 1897 by author, Bram Stoker." Stella hesitated, half closed her eyes. "You're not suggesting –"

Vensing shook his head. "No. However, take this thought on board. According to most reports, Bram Stoker based his mythical Count Dracula on a real-life fiend named Vlad Dracul, better known as 'Vlad the Impaler.'"

"Yes, I know all about his atrocities."

"Okay! Now consider this," Vensing continued. "Are you familiar with the term: Quantum Electrodynamics?"

"Of course," Stella replied. "It's the study of electromagnetic radiation and its interaction with charged particles in terms of Quantum Theory."

"Correct! And the Quantum Theory concerns the behavior of physical systems based on the idea that they can only possess certain properties, such as energy and angular momentum, in discreet amounts."

"Yes, but what's that got to do with –"

"Bear with me," Vensing said. "Quantum mechanics is the branch of mechanics, based on the Quantum Theory, used for interpreting the behavior of elementary particles and atoms, which do *not* obey Newtonian mechanics."

"You'd better get to where this is leading in a hurry. You're losing me."

Vensing tossed off a polite smile. "Every living creature emanates a force belt or energy field," he went on. "And, depending on the metaphysical makeup of the being in question, that energy field will be either positive or negative. When a person dies, that energy field, or spirit if you like, is released from their body. This is a wild idea but, what if, before that energy field can dissipate, it somehow becomes entrapped in an electromagnetic radiation belt and is cast adrift into the ether, maybe even further, into the cosmos, until it finds a suitable host to inhabit. When it does, it can virtually renew its existence. If there is even the remotest possibility that this could happen, and Vlad Dracul's energy field, as it left his body, was trapped in this manner, then –"

Stella remained silent, allowing Vensing's ideas to sift

through the logical compartment of her brain. Soon, she shook her head. "No, it's not logical."

"Logic has nothing to do with what's happening around here."

Stella closed her eyes, thought for a moment, then opened them. "All right, if we accept that your theory does contain an element of fact, then this Count Dal V. Lucard could turn out to be an innocent party who just happens to be unlucky enough to be chosen as host to an evil entity, which may or may not be that of Vlad the Impaler."

"No!" Vensing exclaimed. "I believe that the being, who used to be the Count, no longer exists. This evil force has taken over his body to the extent that I feel it has transformed him into a real vampire. By whatever means it has been achieved, we are dealing with some form of an actual Prince of Darkness."

"And if we kill him, and you're wrong, we will have murdered a guiltless man."

At that point, the old graveyard keeper came running toward them. There was fear in his eyes. Breathing heavily, he muttered, "quickly, Doctor… graveyard… young Larry."

"What? What is it, man?" Vensing tried to calm the old keeper.

"It's Larry… awful," he replied. "He's dead – throat ripped to pieces. And… his girlfriend… she's gone."

Vensing glanced at Stella. "Theory or no theory, I intend to try and stop these horrific crimes."

"Lead on, Hal," Stella said. "I'm with you."

Chapter 4

The scene at the graveyard wasn't one for the faint-hearted. The boy's head was practically severed from his shoulders. His blood, still seeping from his terribly mutilated body, had saturated one side of the vehicle and surrounding earth.

"With so much blood splattered around," Vensing said, "the bastard who did this must have some on their clothes and shoes."

Stella was studying the soft ground. "Possibly, and yet, there are no other footprints apart from those of the young boy."

Vensing pulled at one end of his moustache. "This has happened within the last half hour. I'll get old Arnie here to organize the removal of the body. In the meantime, Stella, how do you feel about paying a visit to Castle Lucard?"

"I think it's an absolutely creepy but wonderful idea. Although, I don't expect we'll find too much."

Vensing cast a long, lustful look over Stella's magnificent body. "It's amazing what you *do* find when you least expect it."

The night seemed to be getting darker with occasional gleams of weird, green-tinted moonlight between the rents of heavy clouds that scudded across the sky. By the time Stella and Vensing reached the stark, imposing walls of the castle, a light rain had begun to fall. Before they could knock on the massive, ornately-carved wooden front door, its rusty hinges creaked as it opened slowly inward.

"Apparently someone knows we are here." Vensing entered warily.

"There must be some sort of automatic sensor system," Stella remarked, searching around for the device. But there wasn't one. "That's odd, I must find out how that was achieved."

They had taken only a few steps into the dark entrance hall before the massive front door slammed shut behind them. They glanced at each other and shrugged. On the floor to their left were two small oil lamps that suddenly flickered into life.

"Neat trick," Stella commented. "Is the Count a part-time magician?"

Vensing didn't answer; he was looking nervously over his shoulder at both their shadows, cast by the light from the lamps, as they appeared to adopt peculiar, independent movements of their own.

Stella's senses went to 'red alert.' She had the feeling someone else was right there with them, but could see no-one.

The place was thick with dust, the floor seemingly inches deep with it. The walls were also heavy with dust, and in corners were masses of cobwebs. Dust had gathered on these giving them the look of old tattered rags. Moving further into the grim surroundings, Stella and Vensing were mentally preparing themselves for some sort of unpleasantness. But they never expected the revolting, malodorous air they soon encountered.

Long disuse of the area had made the air stagnant and

longer. We'd better be leaving."

"No! You cannot!" the Count exclaimed. "I mean, it would be more advisable to stay here for the night." A flash of lightning was quickly followed by a low, whiplash crack of thunder. The storm was increasing in ferocity. Rain, whipped up by a vicious wind, was hammering at the high windows. "Your arrival was not totally unexpected," the Count continued. "Consequently, I took the liberty of organizing your accommodation. Your rooms are prepared."

Vensing glanced at Stella. She nodded.

"All right, Count," Vensing said, "we will gratefully accept your hospitality."

Count Lucard smiled, baring his sharp teeth. "Come; let me show you the way. I am sure you will find your rooms… comfortable."

***

Dear Reader,

For the next few moments you are about to experience the awe and mystery of travelling through a timeless void that leads you from the previous chapter to —

The Author's Note:

Despite her extraordinary mental aptitude and stunning physical appearance, Stella *does* have one blemish. Or, what could be described as, 'human' imperfection. This fact is known only by Commander Cranston Lamont (Stella's immediate superior), Randy and the surgeons involved at the USC headquarters. As part of the preparation for her interplanetary assignment, Stella agreed to the removal of the top joint of the little finger on her left hand. Through intricate micro-surgery, this was replaced with a device called an audio disseminator.

When activated, this device enables Stella to communicate with Randy, who has a similar receiver/transmitter system built into his circuitry. By biting gently on the artificial fingernail, Stella can activate or deactivate the implement. Protected by a hybrid of silicone and synthetic tissue reconstruction, the finger otherwise appears normal. This break in your concentration is merely intended to ease your bewilderment when, on odd occasions, Stella may start talking to her little finger.

Thank you for your patience…

***

Chapter 5

After guiding them to two adjoining bedrooms, Count Lucard, a suggestive glint in his eyes, said, "I will now bid you goodnight. You must excuse me; I have some… unfinished business to attend to." He then seemed to dissolve into the darkness.

Although they were now alone, Vensing still lowered his voice. "There were no visible signs of blood on the Count's clothes or shoes, but I'm still not convinced. I feel there is a dreaded malevolence surrounding him."

"I feel it too," Stella said. "I'm certain his politeness is covering something sinister. Something so unholy, even hell would reject it."

"Okay, that's it! I'm not leaving you alone tonight. Do you mind if I stay by your side?"

"Hal, I insist on it," Stella replied with a sly grin. "Your room or mine?"

Vensing smiled. "Mine has an extremely noisy nervous system. I suggest we stay here in yours." He let his eyes roam over her body. "It has a more inviting… ambience."

Stella glanced admiringly again at the tantalizing bulge in Vensing's pants. "Close the door," she said, "and we'll try to put the unpleasant problems aside for a while. Besides, I can see that you have… something else in mind."

She pulled him close, kissed him and gave a lustful moan as the firmness of his instrument of pleasure pressed against her loins.

"I could be wrong," Vensing said, "but I'm getting the impression you have the same thing in mind."

Stella stepped back and, with slow, sensual movements, eased out of her brief outfit. A roguish grin curled the corner of her mouth. For a few seconds she stood in the classical, relaxed pose of the nude, all the weight on the right leg and the left knee bent and turning slightly inward, her head to one side and hands on her hips, proudly displaying her nakedness. The flickering flame of the oil lamp only served to emphasize the brazen, carnal craving in her eyes. It was an intoxicating moment of raw, sexual enticement that no artist could ever have hoped to capture on canvas.

Without taking her eyes off Vensing, Stella lowered herself onto the bed and began to fondle her full, rounded breasts with one hand while caressing her pleasure zone with the other. Her large nipples were now firm projections; her eyes were ablaze with a fiery yearning as Vensing watched, spellbound by the magnetism of her wanton sexuality. With Stella's magnificent naked body spread-eagled on the bed, her loins already wet with anticipation, Vensing was incapable of restraining himself any longer. He quickly discarded his clothing and stood beside the bed.

Stella gave a squeal of astonishment, her eyes wide as she stared at the impressive dimensions of Vensing's erection. Overcome by a shameless need for the pleasures she knew it could lavish upon her, she took hold of it and issued a passionate demand. "Now, Hal, I need to feel this beautiful weapon of yours penetrating the depths of my loins."

Vensing didn't need to be told twice. He sprang on top

of her, positioned the tip of his aching member at the entrance to her drenched cloven inlet and began to slowly ease into her. As each hedonistic thrust took him further into her soft laboratory of love, Stella felt her nether mouth stretching to its utmost limit. He suddenly flicked his tongue across her nipples. An ecstatic spasm shook her body. She began to lose control, her vaginal muscles contracting from her approaching orgasm. Screaming and thrashing like some wild animal, Stella bit and scratched him as her rapturous release saturated her cavity.

Impelled by her unrestrained screams of passion, Vensing also quickly succumbed to that gratifying rush of ecstatic bliss. Then, delighted that his enormous phallus was still firm, but fully aware that it had not yet gained complete lodgment within her strenuously dilated opening, Stella, moaning with desire, continued her feverish demands. "Give it to me, Hal. I want *all* of it."

This was enough to encourage a renewed invasion. Meeting the energy of his voracious pounding with an equal, fervid appetite, she kept coaxing him to penetrate deeper until, with a mighty thrust, his extraordinary shaft finally became fully sheathed.

Stella lay gasping, panting under him as the agitation of his unremitting column, vigorously stimulating her clit, began to incite yet another climactic inundation. Vensing then groaned loudly as he felt the compression of her warm, surrounding fold drawing from him a further orgasmic surge. Feeling the gush of his sweet nectar flooding the depths of her pummeled cleft of flesh, intermingling with her juices, Stella smiled and gave a satisfied sigh. Immersed in lustful abandon, their inflamed friction continued into the early hours of the morning until, totally drained, they fell asleep in each other's arms.

Chapter 6

The intensity of the storm's downpour had eased to a depressing drizzle. Dawn had turned the lower east sky over Paprika burgh to a dark pink two hours before Stella snapped awake.

She shook Vensing. "Come on, Hal, get dressed. We've wasted enough time. There are murders to solve and missing girls to find."

Vensing frowned as he buttoned his shirt. "I wouldn't have referred to last night as a waste of time." There was dejection in his voice.

Stella kissed him on the cheek. "I'm sorry, that was a bad choice of words. Last night was wonderful and I hope we get the opportunity for a repeat performance. Meanwhile, we need to focus."

"Of course, you're right," Vensing said, getting his mind back to the ghastly crimes. "Hopefully, we can talk the Count into giving us a conducted tour of the castle."

Stella shook her head. "I have a feeling he won't agree to that too easily."

However, their initial search of the main downstairs area revealed no sign of the Count. Vensing called Lucard's name a few times but the only response was the echo of his own voice fading into the cold, stony depths of the old building.

"I would have thought he'd be gracious enough to greet

us for breakfast," Vensing said. "But he doesn't seem to be here."

Stella was silent for a while then said thoughtfully, "If what you are suggesting about Count Lucard is true, it's possible he *is* here – dozing in a coffin somewhere. We need to search this eerie place. But, first, let's head into the village. The mention of breakfast has made me hungry."

At The Frog and Toad pub the air of despondency still hung heavily. And the sight of Stella's scantily-clad body still received a stunned, open-mouthed silence from the locals. Vensing ordered them both a light breakfast. When they'd finished, he gazed into Stella's eyes and asked hesitantly, "Do you... have any one? I mean... are you... romantically involved with any one?"

Stella reached over, put her hand on his arm. Recalling some distant point in time, her eyes glazed as she said softly, "No, Hal, there was someone... someone I loved dearly. We talked about settling down, having kids, all that usual stuff that people in love talk about."

"What happened?"

"It... wasn't meant to be."

"I'm sorry." Vensing quickly added, "I didn't mean to pry."

Stella came back from where her thoughts had taken her and smiled. "Why do you ask?"

Vensing took a moment to answer. When he did, his voice was shaky. "Stella, I was wondering, when all this horrible business is over, if... you might consider staying here, with me?"

Still smiling, Stella's answer was calm, gentle.

"Darling, Hal, what we had last night was something special. It was a night I will never forget. But you don't know anything about me. You are suggesting we begin a lasting relationship based on one night together. And that's the sweetest thing I've heard for a long, long time. I'm incredibly flattered but –"

"But you don't feel the same about me."

Stella decided to confront the situation by telling the truth. "I think you are one of the kindest, handsomest men I have ever met. You are also an amazing lover but, I have a job to do that just doesn't allow me to become romantically attached. Many people on many worlds rely on me. And, because of that, I cannot afford to fall in love." She squeezed his arm. "Can you understand that?"

Vensing smiled but there was sadness in his eyes. "Yes, I understand." He forced himself to change the subject. "Speaking of a job to do, we'd better get back to Castle Lucard. And, just to prepare you, if we do happen to run into trouble, we'll have to deal with it on our own. We cannot expect help from any one in the village."

"Don't worry." Stella sounded confident. "If there's an emergency, I'm sure we'll be able to cope."

It was just after midday. The sky over Paprika burgh hadn't changed from its muted shade of dreary as Stella and Vensing opened the castle's huge front door. Inside, nothing appeared to have changed. Except for the wind swirling dust and dead leaves up against the castle walls, there wasn't a sound. The Count was still nowhere to be seen.

"Where do you think we should start looking?" Vensing asked. "And, by the way, what are you expecting us to find, the missing girls?"

"I hate to say it," Stella replied, "but, yes, at this stage foul. Yet, coming through this, was an earthy smell, as of some dry miasma. It seemed that it was composed of all the ills of mortality and underlined with the pungent, acrid smell of blood. Ordinarily such a stench would have brought an end to their visit, but their crucial purpose gave them the fortitude to continue.

At the end of one of the many corridors, they came upon a door with soft light filtering under it. Stella and Vensing both pushed against it until, with the loud grating noise of neglect, it swung open to reveal a dimly-lit dining room. A large wooden table was set and two oil lamps were burning – one on the table, the other on a bench at the far end of the room.

From the shadows at the opposite end, a tall man suddenly appeared. He was clad all in black including a cape which he held in a way that hid most of his face. They could see only the gleam of a pair of bright eyes, which seemed red in the lamplight, as he turned to face them.

The dark figure motioned them in with a courtly gesture. "Good evening." His voice was deep, cultured, with a strong, old-Earth, European intonation. "I bid you, welcome." He lowered his cape and smiled. The lamplight fell on a hard-looking mouth with extraordinarily red lips, and sharp teeth as white as ivory.

"Good evening, Count," Vensing replied. "Please accept our apologies for arriving in such a manner. Oh, and this is a friend of mine, Stella Starlust."

The strange person glided forward. "I am Count Dal V. Lucard." Then, holding out his hand, he grasped Stella's with a strength that made her wince. The hand was cold as ice. He kept hold of Stella's hand and continued to apply pressure, as if testing her. She didn't miss the faint flicker of surprise on his pale features as she easily matched his vice-like grip.

He released her hand and again said, "I bid you, welcome. I surmise, Dr. Vensing, you have ventured into my... home as protection from the rain. Please, allow me to prepare something for you to eat."

He held a chair for Stella. As she sat down the man leaned over her, his lips close to Stella's bare neck. She then bumped two table knives that spun together forming the shape of a crucifix. Noticing it, a hissing sound, much like that of a snake, escaped the Count's lips and he quickly moved back from the table into the shadows.

There seemed a strange stillness over everything. Then, a wolf began to howl somewhere in the distance, a long-agonized wailing as if from fear. The sound was taken up by another wolf, then another and another, until a wild howling, borne on the wind, appeared to come from all around the castle.

Emerging silently from the shadows, the Count's eyes gleamed. "Listen to them," he said, "the children of the night. What music they make!"

Vensing surreptitiously checked the Count's shoes and clothing but detected no signs of blood. Stella was then startled by an odd optical effect. When the black-caped figure stood between her and the lamp's flame, he didn't obstruct it. Stella thought she could see the lamp's ghostly flicker through the Count's body. The effect was only momentary and Stella decided her eyes were probably deceiving her. "Thank you for your kind offer," Vensing said. "However, we won't prevail upon your generosity any

I am almost certain we are looking for those six, no, make that now seven, missing girls'… dead bodies."

"You believe they are all dead?"

Stella nodded. "We've seen some of upstairs. This place has to have a cellar, or dungeon, or something similar underneath. Let's see what's beyond the cobwebs."

The maze of corridors and passageways seemed to be endless, at times leading back to where they came from, at other times, dead ends. Three, possibly four hours later, they finally found an iron door at the end of one of the passageways. It was bolted but not locked. Opening it, they discovered stone steps leading down into darkness.

"This looks promising," Vensing said. "But it's pitch black down there."

"There was a lamp burning a couple of corridors back," Stella recalled. "I'll get it. You stay here and, don't move!"

She hurried away leaving Vensing staring into the ghostly murkiness. As he waited, he thought his mind must be playing tricks. He imagined he heard the distant clanging of chains coming from below. And then, a soft groan, quite possibly a female's voice. He listened intently but there wasn't another sound. Was it his imagination? Should he wait for Stella to return? Or should he venture into the blackness to see if someone needed his help?

Outside, the daylight had already faded behind the surrounding mountains. Dusk was silently giving way to the approaching twilight and deepening shadows were gradually climbing the castle's high walls when Stella returned with the lamp.

"All right, Hal," she said, "now let's see where this leads."

But Vensing was nowhere in sight.

Chapter 7

"Damn! I told him not to move," Stella muttered. "I wonder if the day will ever come when a male will readily accept a female's advice."

The stone stairway was slippery from dampness and mold. Three times, Stella almost lost her footing. The constant twisting and turning of the narrow passageway was causing Stella to lose her sense of direction. Eventually the passage levelled out and led into a large, sepulchral room. The area appeared to be cut out of the rock shelf that formed the base of the castle. The walls were rock, the floor bare earth and dust. The stench was sickening.

Close to one wall, hanging from the ceiling by chains around their feet, were the naked bodies of seven young girls. Even in the dim light, Stella could see that their throats had been ripped open. Beneath the head of each body, a receptacle was collecting the girls' blood.

Stella moved closer. She noticed one girl's blood was flowing reasonably freely. The body was still warm. This had to be Carla, the last girl who had gone missing. A slight sound came from behind her. Stella turned quickly. The glow of the lamplight was reflected in a pair of red eyes. Below these, two vicious fangs were dripping with blood and saliva – a stark contrast to the rest of Lucard's pale, gaunt features.

The Count laughed. It was a hideous, bone-chilling

laugh. "Starlust, you have made a serious mistake by meddling in affairs that do not concern you."

"Murder concerns me, Count," Stella replied, unfazed by Lucard's intimidating presence.

"Murder? I have not committed murder!" Lucard bellowed. "Just as a wild beast kills its prey to survive, I also kill to survive. I have a continuing need for the uncontaminated blood of young females. It is what has kept me alive for hundreds of years."

Stella was looking for a distraction. "Maybe it's time to think about a retirement plan, before you get too old." There was nothing within reach. To defeat him, it would have to be with her bare hands. "You're actually expecting me to believe you are a vampire?"

"That is one title that applies."

"Vampire or not," Stella said determinedly, "as far as I'm concerned, you're still a murderer and I intend to see that justice is done." She placed the lamp on the ground and braced herself for a physical confrontation.

"I wouldn't be too hasty in attempting anything you might regret." Lucard's voice was low, menacing. "Pick up the lamp and aim its light to your left."

Stella did as Lucard asked and her eyes widened in horror. Hal Vensing was in a standing position, strapped to a steel post. He was unconscious. He was also naked, his hands tied behind him, his feet bound together. A track extended from his feet straight out in front of him. At the other end of this track, about ten feet away from him, a bizarre contraption held an enormous spear, the point of which was aimed directly at Vensing's heart. The mechanism was moving slowly along the track toward

Vensing's defenseless body. Stella figured, at the rate it was travelling, it would take five maybe six minutes to reach him.

"This switch I am holding can stop the device, or instantly release the spear," Lucard said. "The choice is yours, Starlust."

Stella felt helpless. She was too far away from Lucard to attack him, and too far away from Vensing to interrupt the mechanism. She had to face the fact that she was stymied.

"Okay, you cowardly bastard," she spat the words at him. "What is your ultimatum?" Out of the corner of her eye, she saw the spear edging closer.

"Take off your clothing," Lucard replied.

"What?"

"Take off your clothing. I will not repeat it!"

Stella realized she had no choice. She removed her outfit and stood before him, the glow from the lamp highlighted every voluptuous contour of her naked body. She glanced at the spear, a quick mental calculation, possibly three minutes left.

"Come here," Lucard ordered, "I need you close to me."

Again, Stella did as he commanded. *What has this vile creature got in mind?* As she drew nearer, she made the mistake of looking directly into his eyes. Something suddenly happened to her whole being. Her will, as strong as it was, was fighting like never before to avoid a demonic force trying to control it. She felt as if her body was on fire. Her mind was becoming muddled. She could hear Lucard demanding, "You will be mine! Say you will be mine and I will let Vensing live. Come with me. Immortality will be yours. Do not fight it."

Stella could feel herself slipping from reality. His will was overpowering. She had to fight back. Hal! She had to save Hal!

Lucard had his arm around Stella's waist. Her eyes were closing. Through her lashes she saw the wicked, burning desire in his eyes, the moisture on his scarlet lips. Stella felt overwhelming fear. She was losing control to this loathsome fiend. Hal's preservation was drifting from her mind. She saw Lucard lower his head, felt his hot breath on her neck; the sensitive skin on her throat began to tingle from the soft, shivering caress of his lips and the sharpness of two teeth, pausing, just touching.

Consumed by his evil spell, and unable to counteract his will, Stella closed her eyes in ecstasy... and waited.

Chapter 8

Stella could hear Lucard's voice, in her head, all around her, overtaking her senses. "Give in to my will," he was saying. "You are weakening. Stop fighting it. You do not have much time if you wish to save Vensing."

Vensing! The name ignited a spark somewhere within her. If she was to save Hal, she *had* to give in, to become one of the undead, a part of this monster's existence... forever! Then again, she felt Lucard would probably kill Hal regardless. There must be only seconds left.

As Stella felt the Count's fangs beginning to pierce her skin, terrible visions of debauchery, devastation and death came flooding from Lucard's mind into her own. She saw and felt the suffering of countless past victims – thousands upon thousands impaled for disobeying him, their bodies left to rot outside the walls of his kingdom. She saw the nauseating horrors he'd inflicted – people decapitated, others with their eyes gouged out, skinned alive, boiled, burnt, and dismembered...

Stella then realized Hal was right. Encased in the Count's body was the hellish entity of... Vlad Dracul, 'Vlad the Impaler.'

No! Somehow, she had to break free of his control. Summoning what strength and willpower she had left, Stella forced Lucard away. She had him at arm's length, her whole-body trembling from the strain. But it was no use. He was too powerful for her – mentally and physically. His mouth was open, his fangs glistening. Stella saw Lucard's head go back, ready to make the final thrust at her throat.

Suddenly the Count let out a terrifying scream. Stella readied herself for the inevitable. But, instead of lunging forward, Lucard staggered back, his red eyes glaring with a mixture of hate and shock. Stella's mind and body instantly returned to normal, the spell had been broken. It was then she saw why. The Count was thrashing and writhing helplessly. A thick, wooden stake had burst through his chest. Lucard stared in disbelief at the sharp, blood-stained piece of wood protruding from his body. He gave Stella a vindictive look then pressed the switch, releasing the spear.

Stella, anticipating his action, was already racing toward Vensing. The spear was only inches away from him. She heard the mechanism click, releasing the deadly object. With amazing speed, Stella sprang, caught the end of the weapon, diverting it a split second before it smashed into Vensing's chest.

Still holding the spear, Stella fell heavily onto the track between Vensing and the immobilized device. At that moment, Vensing regained consciousness. Puzzled by the fact Stella was lying on the ground, he asked, "What happened?"

Stella smiled and got to her feet. "Lucard made a point that I didn't agree with." She untied Vensing and they moved to where the Count's body was in advanced stages of decomposition. As they watched, the body crumbled into dust, blending inconspicuously with the dirt floor.

"You were right, Hal," Stella said. "Your electromagnetic radiation belt theory proved to be correct. Count Lucard's body was merely a façade for, none other than, the evil entity of, Vlad the Impaler."

"He told you?"

"In a way," Stella replied. "While we were 'necking', his thought waves entered my own. I saw and experienced some of the disgusting cruelty that odious creature was responsible for."

"Do you think that's the end?"

Stella ran her tongue slowly around her lips. "It's definitely the end of the Count. But, as for the spirit of Vlad Dracul, who can tell? Let us hope so."

Vensing took Stella in his arms and kissed her tenderly on the lips. "Thank you, for saving my life and for ridding our village of the hideous monster. By the way, how did you achieve his demise?"

Stella shrugged. "I didn't."

"But who –"

Vensing was interrupted by a metallic voice from the shadows. "My name is Randy. Serial number: 18.15.2.15.20. It is my pleasure to make your acquaintance, Dr. Vensing. Now, please, would you both be so kind as to put your clothes on. It is my electrodes, you see. I suffer with an overheating problem.

After realizing you were in trouble, Starlust, I found you by following the frequency signal from your audio disseminator, which you left on. Perceiving that you were apparently dealing with a vampire, I simply manufactured a wooden stake and did what needed to be done."

"You cut it a bit fine," Stella commented.

"Not at all," Randy replied. "I would suggest that I timed it perfectly."

Stella glanced at the top joint of the little finger on her left hand and frowned. "I didn't know my audio disseminator was on."

"It has been on since last night," Randy said.

"Last night?"

"Last night."

"All of last night?" Stella asked.

"Yes," Randy replied.

"Then, you heard —"

"Everything! Really, Starlust, in future try to be more careful. You *must* consider my electrodes."

Stella smiled. "I'm sorry, Randy; I promise I *will* be more careful."

Vensing shook his head, completely bewildered.

The night sky was clear and a cool, mild breeze seemed to be heralding a new beginning for the curious little village of Paprika burgh. Randy followed at a discreet distance as Stella and Vensing strolled down toward the pub.

"I'll arrange for a decent burial of those poor girls," Vensing said. "As soon as the villagers know that the Count has been vanquished, I'm sure I will get all the help I need. You know, I've just realized something."

"What's that?" Stella asked.

"The Count's name, Dal V. Lucard, if you take the full point as a separation of the two names, spelled backwards, they become, Vlad Dracul."

Stella raised one eyebrow. "Interesting," was her only comment.

When they reached The Frog and Toad, Vensing turned to Stella. There was moisture in the corners of his eyes.

"Will you let me buy you a… farewell champagne?"

"I don't think that's such a good idea, Hal. If I do, I might be persuaded to stay longer, which would only make my departure all the more difficult." She looked deeply into his eyes. "I really do have to go. I'm sorry."

Vensing put his arms around Stella and kissed her with such a tender, loving passion, she had to quell an overwhelming desire to make love to him there and then.

Eventually, he pulled away. "I guess this is goodbye. I'll probably never see you again."

"No-one can predict the future, Hal. There is always a possibility I could receive another distress call from you. And if I do –"

"Last night you touched my heart in a way I have never ever experienced before. It was too beautiful for me to even hope it would last." He wiped away a tear. "No, Stella, I know this is goodbye… forever."

Stella's heart was aching for him. She managed a smile. "Three things the wise man does not do, Hal. He does not plow the sky. He does not paint pictures on the water. And he does not argue with a woman."

Vensing also forced a smile, then turned and walked away.

On their way to the Euphoria, Randy broke the silence. "Another mission accomplished, Starlust."

"Yes," Stella said softly, "another mission accomplished." She shook her head then added, "Randy, I promised myself I wouldn't let any one break into my heart again. That's easy in theory. Hal is a wonderful person, I'll miss him. Last night *was* incredible."

"I know," Randy replied.